Go
Salv

MW01241886

In this epic account, Angeline and Clifton are 2 examples of what it looks like to become a part of "God's process". Backed with scriptural references and painting the picture with Angeline and Clifton, it'll be clear that "God's Process" is truly His process alone. There's much controversy amongst proclaiming believers regarding how someone is saved and what that looks like to walk it out. Hopefully the pages to follow will answer many questions most may have and put to rest any doubts of those that just simply do not know.

God's Process
Salvation is a Journey

Table of Contents

God's Process
Salvation is a Journey

Chapter 1- That sums it up!

"Jesus replied, "I tell you the truth, unless you are born again, you cannot see the Kingdom of God." "What do you mean?" exclaimed Nicodemus. "How can an old man go back into his mother's womb and be born again?" Jesus replied, "I assure you, no one can enter the Kingdom of God without being born of water and the Spirit. Humans can reproduce only human life, but the Holy Spirit gives birth to spiritual life. So don't be surprised when I say, 'You must be born again.'"John 3:3-7 NLT

God's Process
Salvation is a Journey

That sums it up right there! One must be born again to see the Kingdom of God and that's the beginning of the "Salvation Journey". Unfortunately, there's much debate and confusion around this concept and there are many false converts and those proclaiming to be Christians and are not born again in Christ. There's much to say about the traps of religion and the delusions of doctrines, but this account is simply putting forth the true examples of "God's Process" and what it may look like to be born again.

God's Process
Salvation is a Journey

"If you openly declare that Jesus is Lord and believe in your heart that God raised him from the dead, you will be saved. For it is by believing in your heart that you are made right with God, and it is by openly declaring your faith that you are saved. As the Scriptures tell us, "Anyone who trusts in him will never be disgraced." Jew and Gentile are the same in this respect. They have the same Lord, who gives generously to all who call on him. For "Everyone who calls on the name of the Lord will be saved."" Romans 10:9-13 NLT

God's Process
Salvation is a Journey

As the scriptures state, it's about a verbal confession and truly believing in your heart. It's an act of your free will and choosing to sincerely become a follower of Christ. We understand that when most people come to Jesus, they're not this 100% cleaned up and guilt free person. Jesus knows exactly where we are and he provides grace for us every step of the way. The controlling factor is having a sincere heart to keep Him first and not being afraid to confess our faults and repent of our sin when we make mistakes along the way.

God's Process
Salvation is a Journey

"For the word of God is alive and powerful. It is sharper than the sharpest two-edged sword, cutting between soul and spirit, between joint and marrow. It exposes our innermost thoughts and desires. Nothing in all creation is hidden from God. Everything is naked and exposed before his eyes, and he is the one to whom we are accountable." Hebrews 4:12-13 NLT

Jesus understands that we have a fallen nature and some of us may battle with sinful thoughts, habits and desires. This is why he came. Most people don't come to Jesus because of the preconceived notion of religion.

God's Process
Salvation is a Journey

Chapter 2- Religion

Unfortunately religion is one of the most deadly tools used by Satan to keep people away from Jesus and generate an improper image of what it means to be a follower of Christ. To take it a step deeper, Satan is behind many of the unfortunate situations that people go through while working twice as hard to cause those to stand against and ignore their only solution, which is Jesus Christ.

God's Process
Salvation is a Journey

"God sent his Son into the world not to judge the world, but to save the world through him. "There is no judgment against anyone who believes in him. But anyone who does not believe in him has already been judged for not believing in God's one and only Son. And the judgment is based on this fact: God's light came into the world, but people loved the darkness more than the light, for their actions were evil. All who do evil hate the light and refuse to go near it for fear their sins will be exposed. But those who do what is right come to the light so others can see that they are doing what God wants."" John 3:17-21 NLT

God's Process
Salvation is a Journey

"But if we are living in the light, as God is in the light, then we have fellowship with each other, and the blood of Jesus, his Son, cleanses us from all sin. If we claim we have no sin, we are only fooling ourselves and not living in the truth. But if we confess our sins to him, he is faithful and just to forgive us our sins and to cleanse us from all wickedness." 1 John 1:7-9 NLT

It's clear that Jesus is not in the "condemnation business". He simply wants us to come to him so he can clean us up and help us to live fruitful lives and help others.

God's Process
Salvation is a Journey

Anyone that makes God out to be someone other than that, they're providing an improper perspective of God.

God is merciful and he desires mercy. He just simply wants us to love Him through His Son Jesus Christ. Not through man, a church organization, or things that we do to try to prove our love. He just wants us to know Him and the power of His resurrection as the Apostle Paul proclaimed in Philippians 3:10.

God's Process
Salvation is a Journey

Chapter 3-The Kingdom of Darkness

One thing that people have been kept in the dark about is the fact that the kingdom of darkness and demonic spirits are constantly at work. These unseen forces can influence one's thoughts, emotions, actions, speech, and much more. This was in fact alluded to in the Bible.

"I don't really understand myself, for I want to do what is right, but I don't do it. Instead, I do what I hate. But if I know that what I am doing is wrong, this shows that I agree that the law is good. So I am not the one doing wrong; it is sin living in me that does it. And I know that nothing good lives

God's Process
Salvation is a Journey

in me, that is, in my sinful nature. I want to do what is right, but I can't. I want to do what is good, but I don't. I don't want to do what is wrong, but I do it anyway. But if I do what I don't want to do, I am not really the one doing wrong; it is sin living in me that does it." Romans 7:15-20 NLT

"For we are not fighting against flesh-and-blood enemies, but against evil rulers and authorities of the unseen world, against mighty powers in this dark world, and against evil spirits in the heavenly places." Ephesians 6:12 NLT

God's Process
Salvation is a Journey

Until one comes to terms with the fact that we are involved in a spiritual warfare with unseen forces, one will have a close to nonexistent salvation journey. Not saying they're condemned or not born again, but the Word of God has made it clear that we are in fact soldiers once we embark on this salvation journey.

"Endure suffering along with me, as a good soldier of Christ Jesus. Soldiers don't get tied up in the affairs of civilian life, for then they cannot please the officer who enlisted them. And athletes cannot win the prize unless they follow the rules. And hardworking farmers should be the first to

God's Process
Salvation is a Journey

enjoy the fruit of their labor." 2 Timothy 2:3-6 NLT

Being a follower of Christ isn't easy, but it's surely rewarding in this life and the next. *"The thief's purpose is to steal and kill and destroy. My purpose is to give them a rich and satisfying life."John 10:10 NLT*

"For the Son of Man is going to come in his Father's glory with his angels, and then he will reward each person according to what they have done."
Matthew 16:27 NIV

God's Process
Salvation is a Journey

Chapter 4- A leap of Faith

I once heard someone say that it's a leap of faith to believe in God, yet it's also a leap of faith not to believe in God. Either way, faith must be exercised in order to come to the conscious conclusion to choose to believe or not to believe. It's a decision that one must be comfortable dying with and I'd rather die knowing there's hope on the other side. Unfortunately, the kingdom of darkness causes a constant unseen pull away from Jesus.

God's Process
Salvation is a Journey

It's almost as if everyone has a built in antivirus that causes people to shy away from Jesus or anything that has something to do with Him. I know it's the sin nature, but it's also the kingdom of darkness constantly at work. This can be compared to a network, except it's demonic. One thing that gets me is how Jesus' name is the only name blasphemed over any other false religious leader's name. You'll never hear someone say, "O my Muhammad, or O Buddha, or anything like that.

God's Process
Salvation is a Journey

You'll certainly hear people blaspheme the name of Jesus and God night and day at work, in the streets, and just about anywhere there are not born again believers.

I have provided a solid scriptural foundation on what I intend to say in the following words. As it has been alluded to, God is a God of mercy and he desires a relationship with everyone who comes to him. With that being the case, relationships always start out slow and they begin to gradually get deeper and deeper as trust in one another tends to strengthen naturally.

God's Process
Salvation is a Journey

In order for someone to influence or change another person's character, they must spend time together and grow in levels of intimacy. Most people don't tell their deepest and darkest secrets on a first date or when hanging out with a group of peers for the first time; most of the time, it's light and casual conversation.

In many cases, this is how our relationship with Jesus takes off. I understand that Jesus said "If you love me, obey my commandments" or "pick up your cross and follow me". That's very true and He means exactly what he said.

God's Process
Salvation is a Journey

Unfortunately, people take those sayings and use them in a dogmatic fashion to place guilt, shame, and condemnation on those that have not developed that level of a walk with Christ yet. The truth is Jesus knows exactly where each person is in their individual walk with him and no man can determine if someone is to be condemned.

"For there is one God and one mediator between God and mankind, the man Christ Jesus," 1 Timothy 2:5 NIV

"They crush people with unbearable religious demands and never lift a finger to ease the burden." Matthew 23:4 NLT

God's Process
Salvation is a Journey

It's true that religion is a turnoff for most people and I personally believe its Satan's # 1 weapon used to deceive people, while Music being # 2. It's obvious that music is a tool that Satan uses to enslave the masses and bring forth destruction. Yes, it's very damaging and many people are cursed and cause themselves to be put under all sorts of spells; allowing demons to invade their soul and have a field day vicariously through their members. That's understood.

The damnable part of that is when they come to themselves and they want to turn their lives around, they'll have a disdain towards Jesus because of religion.

God's Process
Salvation is a Journey

This is one of the most deceptive traps that could have been thought up and it's going to take God to intervene to save someone that truly wants to be saved.

Let's examine a scenario of what it may look like if someone came to themselves and the steps that I believe the Lord may take them through as a part of His process. Let's meet Angeline.

God's Process
Salvation is a Journey

Chapter 5 –Angeline's Story

Angeline is a 24 year old college student that stays with her parents in Waco TX. She has a boyfriend named Todd that she's been dating for going on 2 months and they're sexually active. She also has 2 friends that she hangs out with regularly named Tasha and Stacy. Living with her parents is very stressful to her because of their high expectations. She lives in a privileged household and her father paid for her tuition at Baylor University to study biochemistry.

God's Process
Salvation is a Journey

Her parents are also heavily involved in their local Baptist church and they're board members with a huge sphere of influence. Angeline literally plays "their" game while living in "their" house and once she is out with Todd, Stacy, or Tasha, she lets her hair down and her true self comes out.

Angeline drinks and does all sorts of drugs. Cocaine, molly, lien, and whatever else she believes she can handle. Having an educational background in biochemistry, she prides herself in knowing exactly what each drug is doing to her in great detail each time she partakes in each substance.

God's Process
Salvation is a Journey

One day she heard that one of her favorite rappers was coming to Houston to host a 2 day concert. Angeline listened to this particular rap artist along with many other rap artists regularly without her parents' knowledge. Angeline had mastered the double life since she was in the 10th grade in high school.

It started when she had her dad drop her off at homecoming and she went to her ex boyfriend's house to have sex and back to the school as if she had been at the homecoming dance the entire time. Ever since that day, she had gotten more and

more skilled with her deception and ways to
hide her double life.

She even attended church with her
parents every Sunday and Wednesday. She
also helped out with church events and even
sang in the choir from time to time during
special occasions.

Anyone looking at her from the
outside would just believe that she's just an
innocent good ol' church girl, but in reality
she's lost and wouldn't know Jesus if he sat
next to her on the city bus. Angeline was a
very skilled opportunist and was able to
analyze and take advantage of every
situation to turn the tables her way.

God's Process
Salvation is a Journey

This keen sense of discernment and attention to detail aided her in several situations in what could have been close call encounters of her exposure.

For example one night she was caught coming into the house around 2:00A.M after visiting her boyfriend. When she came in the side door, her mother was using the bathroom and happened to hear her coming in. Her mother questioned why she was coming in so late and Angeline responded, "I just got a price hike alert on my Gas buddy app and gas is going to go up by nearly $1 by the morning and I needed gas" and then she proceeded to show her mom the gas receipt from getting gas at the pump. Her mom didn't question it because she knew Angeline was the type of person that didn't like wasting money and she took advantage of every deal she could get. She got away that night with one of many of her tactics of deception.

To fast-forward a bit; Angeline is not born again, but yet she's heavily involved in church and living with what appears to be upstanding church members and citizens of Waco TX. Again, it'll be easy to assume that Angeline is the poster child for Christianity, while in fact, she's the complete opposite, but soon to be a poster Child for how God's

God's Process
Salvation is a Journey

Process operates. Days before the 2 day concert in Houston, Angeline was trying to come up with a plan to attend both days of the event and have a few extra recovery days before she went back home. She eventually thought of the perfect plan and it involved telling her parents that she planned to attend a Bible camp in Arkansas for 5 days.

Although the Bible camp was a Zoom bible meeting, she knew her parents wouldn't check and she showed them the registration from her phone and they agreed to let her go. Now that she was clear to move on with her real plans, she connected with Todd, Stacy, and Tasha.

God's Process
Salvation is a Journey

Chapter 6- The Event (Angeline's Story)

The day of the event was chaotic. It was about a 3 hour drive and Todd drove the entire way there. They arrived in Houston around 10:30 P.M and there were people drinking and smoking in the open, blocks away from the actual festival. Marijuana smoke filled the streets as they headed to the event. As they got closer, it appeared to be a huge bottle neck of people trying to get in, but they were not letting people in at the moment as it was already packed to capacity. Therefore people just partied right where they were as if they were actually in the event.

God's Process
Salvation is a Journey

People broke out bongs, alcohol, pills, and all kinds of other substances. Todd proceeded to hand everyone a "molly" pill he got from someone that was passing them out a few blocks back while saying "I ain't ever been anywhere where the drugs are free". Taking advantage of the moment, Angeline, Todd, Stacy, and Tasha, popped the "molly" pills in their mouths and chased it down with a Miller High Life, which they also got for free at the event. Music pounding, people jumping and dancing, small fights breaking out and ending quickly; as the partying just continues. Hours go by and Angeline realizes that she can no longer feel her body. She then starts to panic and realize that she can't even see people's faces.

Everyone looks like clay people jumping up and down and she starts to panic. It has come to light that what she and the others had taken was not in fact a "molly", but a very potent hallucinogenic with a derivative of the drug "acid". Angeline was now on a drug trip that she could not control or minimize the effects. She started crying and screaming "please stop, please stop, please stop," followed up with "help me Jesus, help me Jesus, and help me Jesus" repeatedly.

God's Process
Salvation is a Journey

She could no longer recognize her friends nor could they recognize her as they were on the same drug trip. She started to see images of what appears to be aliens, dragons, and hideous beasts.

One of the beasts noticed her and came up to her and looked her dead in her face as she continued to scream "help me Jesus, help me Jesus, help me Jesus" several times.

The beast then appeared to laugh at her and dissolve into thin air. Angeline then dropped to the ground in fetal position praying and crying and asking Jesus to stop what was going on.

God's Process
Salvation is a Journey

People tripped over and stepped on her as the festival went on, but she was so caught up in crying and praying she didn't even notice it. Another 3 hours went by and she was still on the ground in fetal position, but nearing the end of the drug trip as the effects started to wear off.

She finally stood up and looked around and saw that she could see faces again. She also noticed that the drug effects hadn't worn off completely as she still saw shadows over people and dark specs popping in and out her peripheral vision.

God's Process
Salvation is a Journey

She was very tired, very thirsty and light headed. She just wanted to go to sleep. She finally saw Todd, and he was crying hysterically saying "That wasn't no molly, that wasn't no molly, that wasn't no molly". Angeline told Todd that she wanted to go, but they had to find Stacy and Tasha. Todd told Angeline that Stacy ran off somewhere and Tasha was over on a side of a building lying prostrate with her eyes closed trying to hide on the side of the building. As Angeline started to pan the area for Tasha, she noticed dozens of other people on the ground looking as if they had taken the same thing.

God's Process
Salvation is a Journey

Some people were even foaming at the mouth. She realized this was the worst decision that she could have ever made and she just wanted the situation to be over. Todd eventually pulled himself together and attempted to help Tasha get up so they could go. He reached his hand towards Tasha's and she snatched back and yelled "don't touch me!" "I see your horns devil!" "I'm not going to hell with you!" Todd then proceeded to say "it's me, Todd" "We gotta go". Tasha then said, "If I get up, they'll find me". Todd then said "it's not real, it's the drugs and it's causing us to hallucinate".

God's Process
Salvation is a Journey

She then looked at Todd square in the face and said "F you, Todd!" "You're the one that gave us this mess and now I'm on the ground like I belong in the psych ward!"

Angeline was pleased with Tasha's response because she knew that she was back to herself. Tasha finally got up off the ground and asked "Where's Stacy?" Angeline and Todd both shrugged their shoulders saying they don't know, but Todd proceeded to say "I saw her running in the direction away from the main concert area". Angeline tried calling her phone and it went straight to voicemail.

God's Process
Salvation is a Journey

They started walking in the direction away from the event looking for Stacy, but she was nowhere to be found. They finally arrived back to the car and as Todd and Angeline proceeded to get in the car, Tasha exclaimed "So we just gonna leave her?" Todd replied, "What do you expect us to do?" "Keep looking for her in the midst of all those people?" "She probably hooked up with someone, you know she loose!" Tasha replied "Ain't no way she is with somebody after what you gave us!" "She's probably somewhere terrified, and it's all your fault!" Todd replied "Look, I didn't know ok" "I'm sorry", "I just wanted to take advantage of the freebies and have a good time".

Tasha replied "I see where taking advantage of freebies has gotten us and now we can't find Stacy". Angeline just broke down and started sobbing. "I just wanna go" "I can't stop thinking about those monsters and creatures I saw" while sobbing hysterically. "I can't get the images out of my mind". "Just let me stay in the car and y'all go look for Stacy".

"Todd you need to go help find her because you gave her the drugs' ' Angeline exclaimed. As Todd and Tasha went to go look for Stacy, Angeline stayed behind in

God's Process
Salvation is a Journey

the passenger seat of Todd's car. While

Angeline was alone, she started to be afraid

that she would see those creatures again. She

would have thoughts of the beast that looked

her in the face, would come quickly to the

passenger window and she would see it if

she looked out the window. Angeline looked

at the clock in the car and it showed 4:47

A.M. Angeline thought to herself, it should

be daylight soon and I'll feel much better.

She then started to doze off as she was

extremely exhausted from the traumatizing

experience. As she dozed off to sleep, she

immediately started to have a nightmare. It

was the beast that was staring at her and it

God's Process
Salvation is a Journey

opened her mouth and tried to go inside her mouth, but it couldn't go in. She kept screaming "Jesus, Jesus, Jesus", as the creature attempted to enter her. She then woke up out of the nightmare and started sobbing. She sobbed and sobbed for minutes until she said. "Jesus"..... "I know you're probably real" "I hope you're real and I need your help". "I thought I knew you because I go to church every Sunday and help people, but I need you to help me" "I'm sorry of doing all the bad things I've done and lying to my parents, and having sex and everything else I know is wrong". "I'm sorry Jesus". "Can you please help me; can you

God's Process
Salvation is a Journey

please help my friend Stacy wherever she is?" I'll stop lying and having sex, and doing things I know I shouldn't do", while squeezing out each word as she sobbed.

All of a sudden, she felt a warm sensation in her gut area and she started coughing and mucus started to come up her throat. She immediately opened the car door and started throwing up on the ground. As she was bent over coughing up mucus and whatever else was coming up, she felt a light sensation as if something had lifted off of her. She knew that Jesus had met her that morning and she was touched by the King Himself. She started crying with tears of joy and relief and she realized that Jesus is real

and he actually saved her from the torment

of the creatures that she saw that night and

delivered her from other evil spirits that had

been influencing her for several years.

Angeline had been born again and

experienced a moment of deliverance. She

knew her life would never be the same. As

she stood in the parking lot next to Todd's

car, she wanted to go look for Stacy along

with Todd and Tasha and tell them about

what just happened. She proceeded to start

walking towards the event when she saw

Todd and Tasha heading back to the car with

Stacy trailing them.

God's Process
Salvation is a Journey

Chapter 7- Born Again (Angeline's Story)

Angeline ran up to Todd, Tasha, and Stacy, and started hugging them and telling them "I love you" "I love you all", "Jesus is real"…... "Jesus is really real!" They all looked at her questionably, as if she was still hallucinating.

Angeline asked Stacy "girl, where were you!" Stacy replied, "I started seeing meteors coming, so I bounced". "Then, as I ran I noticed a rabbit on my foot it started crawling up my leg and I fell and tried to get it off" "When I got up, I started running again and I saw an ambulance at a red light and I ran up to the driver and asked him if I

could get in the back to hide from the
rabbits." "They pulled over and had me get
on the gurney and asked me if I was allergic
to anything and if they had permission to
treat me". "They gave me sodium chloride
along with other vitamins and minerals to
help the drugs wear off." "The paramedic
said they had been doing that all night for
those that came across their path and that
someone has been giving out really powerful
hallucinogens; driving people insane".
Tasha said "so much for the freebies Todd".
Todd responded "I'm sorry y'all and I'm
done with this stuff for a minute".

God's Process
Salvation is a Journey

Angeline chimed in "I'm done too and I'm giving my life to Jesus, and ya'll need to do the same". Tasha responded "Ok, look at Ms. Church girl tryna preach at us". "You done had yo come to Jesus' moment and now you expect us to follow suit?" "Girl please, not with all the dirt you done and you really think Jesus is gone forgive you just like that?" Angeline replied "I know I was a fake Christian before, but I'm different now!" "I even feel different" "Tasha, I'm not the same Angeline that I used to be ". "Something happened to me in that car while y'all was gone and I know Jesus did it!"

God's Process
Salvation is a Journey

Tasha replied, "Ok girl, we'll see...."

"Don't be trying to have me cover for you while going over Todd's".

Angeline responded "I won't because Todd is no longer my boyfriend". Todd looked at Angeline, and explained "Are you crazy?" "You gone break up with me because you found Jesus now"? "Ok, I see how it is!" "You can walk home!" "You ain't finna break up with me and catch a ride home". Stacy said "Angeline "is it that serious?" "You and Todd seem like the perfect couple". Angeline responded "To be real, Todd and I were just sex".

God's Process
Salvation is a Journey

"Now that I'm serious about Jesus and he's more real to me than He's ever been in my life, I know the next time I have sex, Imma have to be married". "I'm not saying I'm perfect or better than anyone, but I gotta stay true to what I believe and y'all know that when I believe something I'm true to it". "Haven't I had ya'll backs in tough times and weren't y'all able to rely on me to come through?" "I have concluded that Jesus is real and I'm sticking with it and Imma try to get to know Him more PERIOD!"

God's Process
Salvation is a Journey

"Y'all will always be my friends, but we can't do the same things anymore and I don't know if that's the end of our friendship, but this is the end of me doing things that I know God don't approve of." I love y'all and I'll see y'all around" Angeline then proceeded to walk away. Stacy ran up to Angeline as she started to walk away and gave her a hug. Tasha exclaimed "give it time, we'll see if she for real".

As Angeline walked on the sidewalk downtown Houston, she looked down at her phone and saw that it was 5:38A.M and she had 17% battery left.

God's Process

Salvation is a Journey

She had her charger in her purse, but needed to find an outlet so she could charge her phone and catch an Uber back home. She knew it was a 3 hour drive back home and she was willing to pay the Uber driver $1,000 to get her back home. She eventually came across a 24 hour CVS and was able to stop in and use their outlet to charge her phone and order the Uber home. It ended up costing her $489 to get home and she didn't even care. She was happy to be home.

God's Process
Salvation is a Journey

Chapter 8-Confession (Angeline's Story)

When she got in, her mom and dad asked her about the Bible camp and Angeline just broke down crying and saying "I'm sorry", "I'm so sorry" "Mom and dad; I lied!" while sobbing. She went on to tell them what really happened and how Jesus came to help her and now she's really following him and not just acting like it. She also confessed how she has been lying for many years about her life and the things that she has done. Angeline came all the way clean and pleaded for her parents' forgiveness and they forgave her.

God's Process
Salvation is a Journey

After being born again and committing her life to Christ, there was still a lot that Angeline had to overcome. Not really socializing with people that were serious about God, she never had a good support system that would help her in her walk. She still kept in touch with Stacy and Tasha from time to time, but she and Tasha never hung out. They just spoke on the phone and it eventually became a "Hi and Bye" conversation and their relationship just grew apart. Angeline and Stacy would still go out to the mall and walk around and hit the gym together, but that was the extent of their friendship.

God's Process
Salvation is a Journey

Angeline had a ton of habits that she had to overcome. When she was around Stacy and Tasha, she cursed like a sailor, but when she was home or at church, she knew how to turn it off. The Lord started convicting her each time she cursed and eventually it came to the point she no longer had a desire to curse. Angeline also had a ton of music from her favorite rap artist and other rappers in her phone and The Lord started convicting her when she would listen to their music. It was very difficult to stop listening to the artists that she had grown accustomed to listening to; especially when she was driving somewhere or working out.

God's Process
Salvation is a Journey

It was second nature to throw on one of her old favorite songs. She heard some kids at her church mention some artists they listened to named Lecrae, Flame, Toby Mac, and KB and others. She eventually found some of their songs and replaced her rap collection with the Christian artists. This helped her tremendously because she couldn't get with the gospel music they played at her church at the current stage of her growth. Eventually Angeline gotten authentically involved in her church and she was able to share her experience with someone else that went through a similar situation, but she had been raped by her boyfriend.

In that moment as Angeline was sharing her testimony and counseling the young lady at her church, she found her passion and her calling. She knew she could be an aid to those that are trying to come out of a lifestyle of sexual perversion, promiscuity, having a false identity, and a double life. Over time Angeline was met with temptation to hook back up with Todd and even a guy at her church made a pass at her one night after Bible study, but she stood strong and didn't take the bait. However, Angeline could not stop thinking about Todd and she eventually started to have dreams about him and her being intimate.

Being as resourceful as she is, she asked a couple older ladies at her church and they explained to her the power of soul ties and that she has to verbally confess it and verbally ask the Lord Jesus to break the soul tie.

Once she learned about that she did research on soul ties, covenants, legal rights, and a little in demonology. She went through a verbal renunciation of soul ties, covenants, and legal rights pertaining to everyone and everything she believes she was still connected to old friends, old

God's Process
Salvation is a Journey

boyfriends, zodiac signs, astrology, oaths

she made at school, generational curses,

pacts she made with friends, even habits and

ways of thinking she struggled with. Once

she did that, she felt more things lift off of

her and she felt even more free and lighter.

Eventually years had passed and

Angeline had started her own ministry

within the church and she was also a full

time choir member. She's no longer

transitioning from rap, but has become

accustomed to songs that edified her spirit

and glorified Jesus alone.

God's Process
Salvation is a Journey

"When I was a child, I spoke and thought and reasoned as a child. But when I grew up, I put away childish things."1 Corinthians 13:11 NLT

"Don't be drunk with wine, because that will ruin your life. Instead, be filled with the Holy Spirit, singing psalms and hymns and spiritual songs among yourselves, and making music to the Lord in your hearts. And give thanks for everything to God the Father in the name of our Lord Jesus Christ."Ephesians 5:18-20 NLT

God's Process
Salvation is a Journey

The Story that was presented is just one example of what it may look like if someone goes through God's process. One thing that is clear is that God does not expect anyone to be perfect. Now in the story, it didn't mention Angeline falling back into sin, but one thing that she found out about is that unseen warfare. That's an important part of the salvation process.

Let's look into the life of Clifton as he learns the importance of learning how to obey God regardless of what others think about him and how God's Process has a way of causing everything to work out for Clifton's good.

God's Process
Salvation is a Journey

Chapter 9- Clifton's Story

Clifton lives in a condominium in Akron, OH with his mother Shana and his 2 sisters Clair and Maria. Clifton is a 17 year old senior in high school and he works at Home Depot part time. His mother Shana works at USPS as a mail carrier. Clair and Maria are still in elementary school in the 3rd and 4th grades. Between Clifton and his mother's income, they're able to afford to pay the bills and live a pretty comfortable life.

God's Process
Salvation is a Journey

They're not able to save much as any extra money goes towards his mother's habits of gambling, smoking marijuana, and cigarettes. She regularly plays the lottery; purchases scratch offs, and spends many of her Sundays at the casinos in the area. Clifton's father is not involved in his life because he's currently in prison for selling drugs and having possession of illegal firearms. His name is Nate and when he was not in prison, the streets took up most of his time. When he was able to see Clifton, it was just to give him some money or because his mother needed some help with fixing something around the house.

God's Process
Salvation is a Journey

Clair and Maria have a different father and his name is Dedrick. He regularly comes and get Clair and Maria on the weekends to spend time with them. This allows Shana to have time to herself and Clifton is able to hang out with his friends and help out with the Church that he attends regularly. Dedrick also pays child support which also contributes to Shana's gambling and smoking habits. Between school work, and church, Clifton is constantly busy moving from one task and endeavor to the next.

God's Process
Salvation is a Journey

He has been attending a local church for the past 2 years due to his friend Alley at school. He and Alley met his freshman year in gym class. He accidentally hit her in the face during kick ball when he kicked the ball and it hurled towards the side of Alley's face as she tried to dodge the incoming blow. Clifton profusely apologized and vowed to make it up to her by getting her a soda out the pop machine. Ever since that day, they've been close friends. Shortly after the beginning of their friendship, Alley began to share her faith with Clifton. He heard about being a Christian and stories from the Bible, but his family wasn't the church type.

God's Process
Salvation is a Journey

After that school year, Clifton and Alley started to hang out outside of school during the summer and he started to attend the church she attended all her life. Clifton had gotten pretty involved and he accepted Christ as his Lord and Savior his sophomore year after attending a baptismal service at a local park. Clifton was very serious about his faith, but his immediate environment was not conducive to his spiritual growth. There was always some kind of drama playing on the television. If it wasn't Maury Povich, it was Jerry Springer, the local news or some other reality TV show that his mother watched on the regular basis.

God's Process
Salvation is a Journey

Their home constantly smelled like marijuana and cigarette smoke. His mother recently started smoking in the car because Maria's doctor told her that the smoke is affecting Maria's asthma and causing it to worsen. Although his mother smoked in the car, she still carried the stench inside the home and the aroma filled the atmosphere to the point that one could catch contact for being in the area she was sitting. Clifton has made countless attempts to share his faith with his mother and invite her to church with him. She would always respond with something like "What you know about that white Jesus"?

God's Process
Salvation is a Journey

Chapter 10- Brainwashed? (Clifton's Story)

"You letting them brainwash you and you betta not be giving them no money". It was clear that Shana was not interested in Clifton's faith and she even took verbal jabs at him for trying to share it with her. Clifton just did what he could and shared his faith with his younger sister Clair and Maria whenever his mother wasn't around. As Clifton started to grow in his faith, he started to learn more about his situation and why things were the way they were regarding his father, his mother, their financial situation, and his mother's habits.

God's Process
Salvation is a Journey

He started to learn more about discernment of spirits, generational curses, demonology, deliverance, and spiritual warfare. Being a senior in high school with the spiritual insight he possessed, left him on an island alone mentally. Even Alley was not spiritually mature enough to understand some of the things Clifton would explain to her because she was just simply not as disciplined in her prayer and fasting life as Clifton was. During the summer of Clifton's junior year, Clifton came across a book that taught him the importance of fasting and prayer.

God's Process
Salvation is a Journey

The book talked about praying daily and using warfare terminologies and proclamations against evil spiritual forces. Clifton also picked 2 days out the week to regularly fast. He would either do a full day fast or a partial fast depending on what he believed he should do, but he chose to do some kind of fast on Saturday and Sunday. When he started to regularly practice fasting and prayer, his spiritual maturity skyrocketed. Clifton started to have dreams, visions, and revelations about particular situations.

God's Process
Salvation is a Journey

He even became well versed with his gift of discernment and he could discern what spirit was in operation in his mother at times. With all that being said, everything that Clifton had gone through and learned was going to lead him up on one particular situation in life in which he had to make a choice to obey his Heavenly Father and stand on his faith or bow down to his domineering mother and heed to her wishes as a situation was afoot that challenged his faith. As Clifton has been practicing his faith with prayer and fasting, he noticed that his home had become more hostile and tense.

God's Process
Salvation is a Journey

He noticed that his mom started snapping on him and his sisters and she would smoke more and gamble more. There would be nights where she would go to the casino and gamble away bill money and they would end up past due on something and receive shut off notices in the mail. He knew that was outside his mother's character because she had a stopping limit every time she went, all the bills were paid beforehand, and she never would gamble with "bill money". He knew something was stirring in the spirit realm. One night when his mom got home from the casino after losing big, she started to verbally attack Clifton.

God's Process
Salvation is a Journey

Chapter 11-The explosion (Clifton's Story)

"Hey Cliff, what you been doing boy"? "You've been mighty quiet around here, is there something you wanna tell me?" Clifton responded, "Naw ma, I just been really busy with school and church" "You know me; I don't really be up to nothing besides that". His mom responded "Something been off around here for the past couple months and it don't feel right when I come into my own house!" "I been losing money left and right and for some reason when I get here, I just can't stand to be in my own home!" she exclaimed.

God's Process
Salvation is a Journey

Clifton immediately discerned he was talking to an unclean spirit; influencing his mother's thoughts and words. He then responded "You need to get saved ma", "I love you ma and I want you to come to church with me and learn more about Jesus". His mom responded "Saved?!" "F yo white Jesus boy!" "Where was yo white Jesus when yo daddy and his friends got me drunk and raped me?" "Where was yo white Jesus when I had to walk to the hospital when my water broke when I was pregnant with yo a** because yo daddy broke my phone and left me at home to go be with somebody else!"

God's Process
Salvation is a Journey

"I don't know if Nate is yo real daddy anyway because it could be him or 3 other guys because I got pregnant after they all raped me". The words cut through Clifton and he began to tear up. His mother then proceeded to say "F yo white Jesus and you betta not mention him again in this house!" She then stormed to the kitchen to get some wine she kept in the refrigerator. Clifton stormed off to his room and dove on his bed and started to cry out to God begging Him to help him in the traumatic moment.

God's Process
Salvation is a Journey

Eventually Clifton dozed off to sleep as he cried and prayed profusely. When Clifton awoke the next morning, he started to recall the situation that had taken place the night before and he recalled everything his mother had said to him. He started to think about how it could have gone differently had he tried to take authority over the evil spirit that was influencing his mother and tried to cast it out. Then he thought about the sons of Sceva story in the Bible and how they were beaten by demons until they were naked and they ran out the house. Then he recalled a teaching regarding legal rights and how demons have legal

God's Process
Salvation is a Journey

rights to people that are unrepentant. He then thought about what she said about his father and his friends raping her and how she doesn't know if Nate is his biological father. Clifton then started to pray "Heavenly Father........" "You know my thoughts, you know my troubles, and You know my heart and the heaviness upon me". "I need help God". As tears rolled down his face and as he started to sob "God please help me!" "Please help ma" "She need you and I dunno what to do" "God I dunno how to deal with this situation with my dad and I don't even care to know, but whatever effect it has on me please deal with it God"

God's Process
Salvation is a Journey

"Please help me; please help me, in Jesus name! Amen!" What had transpired over the past couple months was intense spiritual warfare. As Clifton started to pray and fast, the demonic realm was stirred to a frenzy and caused his mother to react based on the demons in her manifesting and trying to interrupt Clifton from his prayer and fasting life. This can be also explained as 2 opposing altars being raised in the same house. As one altar is for God Almighty and His Kingdom and another altar is for Satan and his kingdom, there's going to be a constant battle with the close proximity of the 2 opposing kingdoms.

God's Process
Salvation is a Journey

This is alluded to as Clifton being an altar for Jesus and the Kingdom of God and his mother Shana being an altar for Satan and the kingdom of darkness. It's all about physical representation of each kingdom, as spirit beings can only live vicariously through the members of a human being. Clifton had a situation on his hands and he was crying out to God for guidance. There's no one in his life that he could turn to for guidance or advice with how to deal with the situation. The only thing he could do was what he learned from the Bible, books he read regarding spiritual warfare, and taking things to the Lord in prayer.

God's Process
Salvation is a Journey

He felt the Lord impress upon his spirit the verse Isaiah 40:31 NKJV. It says, *"But those who wait on the Lord Shall renew their strength; They shall mount up with wings like eagles, They shall run and not be weary, They shall walk and not faint."* Clifton was uplifted by the scripture and proceeded to go about his day, knowing that God has a plan in store for him. Clifton continued to pray, fast, and study his Word as he went to school and work. He didn't mention Jesus to his mother as she demanded, but he regularly prayed for her. Two weeks later, his mom came home from work early.

God's Process
Salvation is a Journey

Chapter 12- Not Feeling Well (Clifton's Story)

She stated that she wasn't feeling well and that she's going straight to bed. Clifton asked her if she needed anything and she said she just wanted to go to bed. Clifton honored her request and let her go to bed as he watched Clair and Maria for the night. He helped them with their homework and made sure they were all set for the next day for school before they went to sleep for the night. The next morning, Shana was not any better. In fact, she had started to worsen in her symptoms. When Clifton woke up for school he noticed that no one else was up.

God's Process
Salvation is a Journey

His mom normally wakes up Clair and Maria for school first thing in the morning because it takes a long time to get them ready. Clifton knew something wasn't right when his mom wasn't up yet. He went and knocked on the door and he didn't get an answer. He proceeded to say "Ma..... Are you up" "Clair and Maria need to get ready for school". He then waited for a response and the room held silent. Clifton then opened her door and saw that she was in the bed still. He went up to her and started to shake her as he said "Ma, wake up" "We gotta get Clair and Maria ready for school." He then noticed that she was very pale and

God's Process
Salvation is a Journey

she looked as if she wasn't breathing.

Clifton started to panic. "Ma!" "Wake up

ma!" "Are you ok ma" as Clifton shook her

profusely. His mother then opened up her

eyes and looked at him and said "I'm ok

son; I just need to get some rest". Clifton

replied "You slept all night ma!" "You need

to go to the hospital". She responded with

"now you know I don't do hospitals boy and

you betta not call the ambulance". His

mother Shana detested hospitals as she don't

trust doctors nor does she want anyone

running blood tests on her because she's

very nervous about people knowing that she

does drugs. Clifton responded and said

God's Process
Salvation is a Journey

"Well what are we going to do about Clair
and Maria." She replied "Call Dedrick and
tell him to come get them and keep them for
a couple days.......I gotta get some rest".
Clifton responded "ok, but I'll be back to
check on you."Clifton called Dedrick and he
was eager to get his girls for a couple extra
days. Clifton then went to wake Clair and
Maria up and get them ready to go with their
father and he arrived approximately 30
minutes later to pick them up. Clifton went
to check on their mother and she was back
to sleep. He then felt the urge to pray for
her. Clifton kneeled at his mother's bedside
and proceeded to pray to the Lord on her

behalf. "Lord please help my mother" he started to pray along with other petitions on his mother's behalf. He was praying for approximately 5 minutes when he felt the Holy Spirit prompt him to start praying in tongues. Clifton learned the importance of praying tongues throughout his walk with God and that it's a very powerful and effective way to pray. As he prayed in tongues, he started to notice his mother's hand shaking. He realized that he was attacking the kingdom of darkness over her life. Clifton then arose to his feet and started praying with more intensity in the Holy Spirit and started to add words of rebuke and

God's Process
Salvation is a Journey

defeat to the kingdom of darkness. He

prayed like that for another 10 minutes and

he started hearing his mother crying. It

caught him off guard because he never heard

her cry like that before and he knew it had

something to do with him praying. He then

continued praying against all the demonic

forces that were over her life. "I bind you

and cast you out in the name of Jesus" He

yelled "All powers of witchcraft, sorcery,

and divination, I break your power, and I

cast you out in the name Jesus!" "Every evil

altar built against my mother's life, be

destroyed by fire in the name of Jesus."

God's Process
Salvation is a Journey

He prayed many such prayers in high intensity and eventually he noticed his mother convulsing in the bed and coughing up mucus and other substances. Clifton ran and grabbed a waste basket as he was familiar with deliverance as people commonly threw up during moments of deliverance. His mother was going through deliverance and healing. What Clifton didn't know at the time was that his mother was fighting for her life and she had contracted a deadly virus that caused her not to be able to breathe along with other flu-like symptoms.

God's Process
Salvation is a Journey

Chapter 13- Jesus the Fixer (Clifton's Story)

As she laid in the bed, she was passing between life and death and she noticed the spirit realm started to open up to receive her spirit, but her son was praying for her because had she passed at that current moment, she was not going to Heaven to be with God. She was going to go to hell and she realized that. As she laid there as her son prayed, she just consciously agreed with the prayer and it had the same effect as if she was praying along with him. During that experience she experienced the love of Christ and she accepted him during that moment of her near death experience.

God's Process
Salvation is a Journey

When Clifton looked at his mom, he noticed that she was crying and that she looked like she had gained her strength back. She proceeded to say "He is real". "Jesus is real". "Thank you for not giving up on me son and thank you for praying for me". "You were right about everything and I'm so sorry for everything I said". Clifton hugged his mother as tears streamed down his face saying "I love you ma". "I just know that Jesus can fix us all!"

Clifton and his mother grew closer from that experience. She allowed him to talk to her about Jesus. She eventually started attending the church with Clifton.

God's Process
Salvation is a Journey

While growing in her faith was still in "God's Process." She still struggled with cigarettes and cursing, but she eventually was able to break free from those habits as well. Years passed and Clifton, his mother Shana, and his sisters Clair and Maria had become more involved with the church and helped in many capacities. They also incorporated God in the lives at home and even hosted Bible studies from time to time.

In this story, Clifton was faced with the challenge to stand faithful in his mother's home. Still being in high school, he's a rare case of someone dealing in this level of spiritual warfare and spiritual knowledge. God is not a respecter of persons and he speaks to anyone that has faith. The prophet Samuel in the Bible is the best example of this case (1st Samuel Chapter 3).

With both examples, it's clear that Jesus didn't just die to give us an avenue back to our Heavenly Father, but his death also gives us access to power to live a fruitful and successful life here on earth. Unfortunately many professing believers don't know how to successfully war against the entities that are preventing people from having successful lives in our world today.

God's Process
Salvation is a Journey

We are in a spiritual war with unseen spiritual forces and a common argument amongst believers today is if a Christian can have a demon or not. I have concluded that truly born again Christians can have a multitude of demons dwelling in their soul as they profess Jesus to be Lord. In fact, Christians are the only ones eligible to have the demons cast out of them because they'll have the Holy Spirit to keep them from coming back.

God's Process
Salvation is a Journey

" "When an evil spirit leaves a

person, it goes into the desert, seeking rest

but finding none. Then it says, 'I will return

to the person I came from.' So it returns and

finds its former home empty, swept, and in

order. Then the spirit finds seven other

spirits more evil than itself, and they all

enter the person and live there. And so that

person is worse off than before. That will be

the experience of this evil generation." "

Matthew 12:43-45 NLT

God's Process
Salvation is a Journey

One must verbally renounce certain acts, habits, thoughts, and people to be free. This may even need to be done publicly depending on the nature of the renunciation. One also must refrain from all known sin or habits that will open the door to allow the demons back into their lives. Unfortunately, this powerful step is overlooked and treated as if it's not necessary when in fact it's a pivotal point of one's salvation journey. *"Afterward Jesus found him in the temple, and said to him, "See, you have been made well. Sin no more, lest a worse thing come upon you." John 5:14 NKJV.*

God's Process
Salvation is a Journey

Doing this or not doing that can be the difference in falling back into sin, or not being able to progress in life, or becoming discouraged in the salvation journey.

For whatever reason, if someone does fall back into sin, they have an advocate. *"My dear children, I am writing this to you so that you will not sin. But if anyone does sin, we have an advocate who pleads our case before the Father. He is Jesus Christ, the one who is truly righteous." 1 John 2:1 NLT.*

God's Process
Salvation is a Journey

This by no means provides a license to sin; it's simply grace that Jesus provided for when we mess up. Let's let Romans deal with that common delusion. *"Well then, should we keep on sinning so that God can show us more and more of his wonderful grace? Of course not! Since we have died to sin, how can we continue to live in it? Or have you forgotten that when we were joined with Christ Jesus in baptism, we joined him in his death? For we died and were buried with Christ by baptism. And just as Christ was raised from the dead by the glorious power of the Father, now we also may live new lives." Romans 6:1-4 NLT*

God's Process
Salvation is a Journey

We do not want to frustrate the Grace of God, nor try to run game on Him. He sees right through us and knows when we're sincere or if we're just a liar.

"Dear friends, if we deliberately continue sinning after we have received knowledge of the truth, there is no longer any sacrifice that will cover these sins. There is only the terrible expectation of God's judgment and the raging fire that will consume his enemies." Hebrews 10:26-27 NLT

God's Process
Salvation is a Journey

Chapter 14-There you have it!

There you have it folks. It's abundantly clear that we are to exercise our free will to abstain from sin and God has provided us with the necessary tools and resources to do so. Again, we're not expected to be perfect, but we are supposed to come to God with a genuine pure heart and try our best to serve and please Him!

This is also the reason for this book. A lot of born again believers are not familiar with breaking curses, spiritual warfare, deliverance, or anything supernatural about the Bible.

God's Process
Salvation is a Journey

"But Christ has rescued us from the curse pronounced by the law. When he was hung on the cross, he took upon himself the curse for our wrongdoing. For it is written in the Scriptures, "Cursed is everyone who is hung on a tree." Through Christ Jesus, God has blessed the Gentiles with the same blessing he promised to Abraham, so that we who are believers might receive the promised Holy Spirit through faith."
Galatians 3:13-14 NLT

We still need to exercise our authority Christ has given us and break all the curses from off of our lives along with

God's Process
Salvation is a Journey

any soul ties, ungodly covenants and have

demons cast out.

"Look, I have given you authority

over all the power of the enemy, and you can

walk among snakes and scorpions and crush

them. Nothing will injure you. But don't

rejoice because evil spirits obey you; rejoice

because your names are registered in

heaven."" Luke 10:19-20 NLT *"But you will*

receive power when the Holy Spirit comes

upon you. And you will be my witnesses,

telling people about me everywhere—in

Jerusalem, throughout Judea, in Samaria,

and to the ends of the earth."" Acts of the

Apostles 1:8 NLT

God's Process
Salvation is a Journey

He gave us the Authoritative power and the Dunamis power, but it's up to us to allow him to exercise that power through us. There are so many doctrines out there that preach a complex gospel, when in fact it's very simple. *"But I fear, lest by any means, as the serpent beguiled Eve through his subtilty, so your minds should be corrupted from the simplicity that is in Christ." 2 Corinthians 11:3 KJV*

"Now the Holy Spirit tells us clearly that in the last times some will turn away from the true faith; they will follow deceptive spirits and teachings that come from demons. These people are hypocrites

and liars, and their consciences are dead."

1 Timothy 4:1-2 NLT

"For if someone comes to you and preaches a Jesus other than the Jesus we preached, or if you receive a different spirit from the Spirit you received, or a different gospel from the one you accepted, you put up with it easily enough."2 Corinthians 11:4 NIV

It's clear that there are other spirits preaching another gospel while using the same name "Jesus".

God's Process
Salvation is a Journey

I'm not going to go down the list of these gospels that I believe are of another spirit, but one thing I will say is get to know Jesus for yourself and do not follow a human. *"Owe no one anything except to love one another, for he who loves another has fulfilled the law."Romans 13:8 NKJV*

The salvation Journey is indeed a supernatural one and no human being dictates how God chooses to navigate someone through their Salvation Journey.

God's Process
Salvation is a Journey

The individual may listen to someone that may be considered a false teacher or listen to a Christian version of a music genre like Christian rap or Christian rock, and that can be used to get them to their next place in their Journey. It's about what's being produced in that individual at their particular growth stage from that teacher or the musician. It's not up to man to decide where someone is, but its man's duty to preach truth expressed with the fruit in a way it can be received.

God's Process
Salvation is a Journey

Chapter 15- Conclusion

In a perfect world, one would just use 100% Bible scripture with the Holy Spirit, but God allows other vessels to pour into His people and produce fruit for His Kingdom. Here are some books that have helped me. *"The Secret to Success"* by Dr. Eric Thomas, *"101 Weapons of Spiritual Warfare"* by Dr. D.K. Olukoya, *"The Battle of Alters"* by Dr. Francis Myles, *"Monitoring Spirits"* by Prayer M. Madueke, *"Forgiving What You Can't Forget"* by Lysa TerKeurst, *"Healing The Wounded Soul"* by Katie Souza, *and* *"Sustained Fire"* by Dr. Stella Immanuel.

God's Process
Salvation is a Journey

The mentioned teachers have much more offer other than the books I mentioned. Take the time to look them up and see additional videos, teachings, and content they have produced that may be able to help you in your journey.

The Gospel isn't to be used by man to beat someone over the head with. God already gave the law as a school master, law enforcer, and disciplinarian. The Holy Spirit is the school teacher. *"But when the Father sends the Advocate as my representative— that is, the Holy Spirit—he will teach you everything and will remind you of everything I have told you." John 14:26 NLT*

God's Process
Salvation is a Journey

We must endure through the Journey all the way to the end! *"I have fought the good fight, I have finished the race, and I have remained faithful. And now the prize awaits me—the crown of righteousness, which the Lord, the righteous Judge, will give me on the day of his return. And the prize is not just for me but for all who eagerly look forward to his appearing."2 Timothy 4:7-8 NLT "Sin will be rampant everywhere, and the love of many will grow cold. But the one who endures to the end will be saved." Matthew 24:12-13 NLT*

God's Process
Salvation is a Journey

""The Spirit of the Lord is upon Me,

Because He has anointed Me To preach the

gospel to the poor; He has sent Me to heal

the brokenhearted, To proclaim liberty to

the captives And recovery of sight to the

blind, To set at liberty those who are

oppressed; To proclaim the acceptable year

of the Lord.""

Luke 4:18-19 NKJV

By: DeMarquis LaMicheal Jones

a.k.a Marq Jones

God's Process
Salvation is a Journey

"And then he told them, "Go into all the world and preach the Good News to everyone. Anyone who believes and is baptized will be saved. But anyone who refuses to believe will be condemned. These miraculous signs will accompany those who believe: They will cast out demons in my name, and they will speak in new languages. They will be able to handle snakes with safety, and if they drink anything poisonous, it won't hurt them. They will be able to place their hands on the sick, and they will be healed.""

Mark 16:15-18 NLT

Made in the USA
Middletown, DE
15 June 2022